The Wish Fairy

The Basket Of Wishes

An original children's story
By Sandra Reilly

First Printing 2015
Copyright © 2015 by Sandra Reilly

www.sandrareilly.com

Library of Congress Cataloging-in-Publication Data
Reilly, Sandra/The Wish Fairy: The Basket of Wishes

Summary: Magical adventures of a bungling Wish Fairy and her friend Hope.
ISBN 978-0-9964299-1-7

I. Reilly, Sandra 1948- II. Title TXu 1-919-036
III. Book Covers VAu 1-182-649

This story is dedicated to my loving Aunt Virgie who passed on to me her ability to believe in magic.

To my loving Aunt Marlene, thank you for all your love and support. Your encouragement was the catalyst that made *The Wish Fairy* possible. And I want to thank my darling daughter Katie for all the endless hours she put into helping me make these stories the way I had always envisioned them to be. I am forever grateful to these two wonderful women.

Before you begin.....

Throughout my Wish Fairy book series, you will come to love the little girl named Hope. I would like to tell you a little bit about her so you can get to know her better.

She lives in upstate New York with her mom. She is a country girl with a very active imagination and is a firm believer in magic. Hope is a very loving and caring eight year old who loves her flowers of the field, and for good reason. You will also come to know her as a good friend of Misty, the Wish Fairy (a sometimes not so perfect, always-getting-into-trouble kind of fairy). Whenever Misty is in trouble, she always goes to Hope for help.

Another character you will meet in this series is Hope's mom. Mom is a down to earth, hard working woman. She has faith in her daughter but needs some time to believe that magic really exists. Pure of heart, she becomes a true fighter for what is right and truthful. She gives Hope advice, and together they help Misty get out of trouble.

In this story, you will meet a little girl named Francesca, her grandmother Sophia and a young man named Franco. All of these characters will be part of a wonderful wish-granting adventure for Misty.

The Wish Fairy

The Basket of Wishes

Sandra Bailey

Hope was a dreamer; she looked at things differently than everyone else. She knew that magic existed, and many other people were believers now because of her. It wasn't always that way.

Hope had a best friend in a little fairy named Misty. In a very exciting adventure, Hope and her mom helped Misty to become a Wish Fairy. Being a Wish Fairy is a very important job in the fairy kingdom.

People would come from all over the town to listen to Hope tell stories of the fairies who lived under the ground. They were responsible for all the magic that took place there—the flowers that were forever blooming in all their brilliant colors of pinks, purples, blues and yellows in the spring and summer. In fall they would erupt into a blaze of reds, oranges and gold. There was no denying the beauty of the butterflies that lived there. Magically, there were no two alike, each one more beautiful than the next.

Hope was very happy now that others understood and believed in magic. Every night she would sit by her window thinking about Misty. Her mother would come into her room, and they would sit quietly and look up at the stars. She missed her little fairy friend so much.

On one particular night, the stars were putting on a spectacular show, twinkling and shining. They looked like someone had drawn them brilliant white against a dark night sky. Yawning, Hope suddenly felt very tired, kissed her mom and tumbled into bed.

Hope was up early the next morning. She could hear the birds singing outside her window. The rays of the sun felt warm on her face as she lay there. Hope jumped out of bed, got dressed, raced to the back door and pushed it open. Holy Fairy Dust! What a beautiful day. As she stepped out onto the porch, her mother stopped her.

"Where are you going in such a hurry, young lady?"

"I am going to take a walk in the wildflower field. I have been wanting to visit the spot where Misty and the other fairies disappeared on the day she was chosen to be the Wish Fairy. The day we were allowed to speak to the Queen and her High Council for Misty!"

"I remember very well, Hope," said her mother. "I also remember how you love to run off and play without having breakfast, so I packed you this little picnic basket to take with you. Promise me that you will take time to eat."

"I will, Mom! I promise." Hope took the basket and left. She walked until she came to the large rock with the baby soft green moss growing on it. The rock was shaded by a huge old oak tree. It was in the branches of the tree where Misty's mother comforted her after the Council meeting.

Hope sat down on the red and white picnic cloth her mom had packed and gazed down at the spot where she saw the magic for the first time. She remembered how beautiful everything was far below the surface where the fairies lived. She thought about the unicorns with their crystal horns and colored manes.

She could never forget the Queen's castle with the towers reaching up into the clouds or the tiny white doves that playfully chased each other in and out of the tower windows. However, it was the sky that really amazed her. It was so clear and blue that it almost hurt her eyes to look at it.

Hope was starting to get hungry, so she reached down to get her picnic basket. As she grabbed the handle, her hand brushed up against something that was lying in the tall grass next to it.   She couldn't imagine what it could be. "Holy Fairy Dust!" Hope exclaimed. Just sitting there was another basket. This one was much smaller and had a red ribbon attached to the handle with the name Misty painted on it. Hope very carefully picked it up, not knowing what was inside. She shaded her eyes against the sun and looked around the field to see if anyone else was here that might have left it.

When she opened the lid and looked inside, she was surprised to see little pieces of paper. After reading one or two of the notes, she stood up and dropped the basket. Her hands were shaking and her heart was pounding. Small beads of sweat were forming on her forehead. Holy Fairy Dust, she knew what this was!

This basket she found belonged to Misty, the Wish Fairy, and it contained wishes from people from all over the world. Two questions popped into Hope's mind. Why was the basket left here, and how was she supposed to get it back to Misty?

Hope quickly headed for home. She needed to think and to show the basket to her mom. Mom would certainly know how to help, as she had helped her many times before when her problems seemed too big to solve.

But when she got home, her mom was visiting with a neighbor. Hope went to her room. She decided that there was not much she could do tonight, and she really needed to think this through anyway. Morning would be soon enough to talk to her mom. She fell into a very troubled sleep, tossing and turning all night long. She was worrying about Misty and her lost basket of wishes, and thinking about one very important wish she had read from the basket.

It seemed that this wish needed the attention of the Wish Fairy, and quick. It was from a young girl living in a small village in Italy. Her name was Francesca, and she lived there with her mother, father, twin baby brothers and her grandmother Sophia. They were not a rich family, but her father farmed their land and sold his crop to the villagers. Francesca's grandmother was a baker and made the most delicious bread and the most beautiful cakes for the villagers and all the nearby villages. People would come from miles away to buy her yummy, mouthwatering creations.

Francesca's father was a very hard worker but recently had an accident that was going to keep him out of work for a very long time. There would be no more new planting this year. Her mother could not do much to help pay the family's bills, because she had to care for the new babies. Francesca helped her can some peaches and sell them at a little roadside stand. However, it was Francesca's grandmother Sophia who was the one that kept the family strong. As long as she could bake, she would be able to take care of her family.

And then tragedy struck. A worker at the bakery left a candle burning in the kitchen, and before anyone realized what was happening, the bakery burned to the ground. The firemen fought the fire as hard as they could, but it was just too far gone. They left the bakery with tears in their eyes, because they knew what Sophia's bakery meant to her family and the whole village.

On top of that, Sophia's granddaughter Virginia was going to be married in three months. Grandmother Sophia had the most spectacular wedding cake planned for her. After all, the entire village would be there, as well as family from all over the country. It was to be the most beautiful cake anyone would ever see. But without her bakery, she would no longer be able to bake it. The family kitchen was barely big enough for them to sit together for a meal.

Francesca's wish was simple. *I am a believer*, thought Francesca, as she called upon the Wish Fairy to make her see how important it is that she granted the wish. *I wish for a new bakery for Grandmother Sophia.*

Hope woke up with Francesca on her mind. She knew that she had to do something and fast. Three months is not a very long time. She found her mother in the kitchen making breakfast. "Good morning, Hope. I'm making your favorite, blueberry pancakes!" She knew Hope loved to eat the fresh blueberries that grew on the edge of the wildflower field.

"Good morning, Mom. Thank you very much, but I'm not really hungry this morning."

"Why, honey? What's wrong? It is not like you to pass up blueberry pancakes."

"I have something very important to talk to you about, and it really can't wait!"

"Come sit down, Hope. Eat with me, and we can talk." Hope was a little hungry after all. As they ate their breakfast, her mom said, "Okay, now tell me what has got you so upset."

As soon as Hope started to speak, she could feel relief wash over her. She told her mom all about Misty's basket and what was in it. By the time she finished talking, Hope had big tears rolling down her cheeks. Her mom took her into her arms and gave her a big hug. Wiping the tears from her eyes, she told Hope to go and get the basket so she could see it.

Watching Hope walk away, her mom thought what a brave and caring daughter she had. Now she had to come up with a plan to help her.

Deep down beneath the wildflower field, things were not going well for Misty. Being a Wish Fairy was harder than she thought it was going to be. It took every bit of her concentration to be a good one. It was easy to lose track of what you were doing if you didn't pay attention every minute! The past couple of weeks were very difficult, and she had a whole basket of wishes she needed to try and grant.

The Council of Fairies was getting ready to meet. This was when the Wish Fairies gathered to talk about the wishes that they did or did not grant. Misty wanted to be ready. She wanted everything to be perfect—nothing could go wrong.

But, suddenly, Misty had the feeling that something was actually terribly wrong.   Oh, where was her basket of wishes?

"I knew I had it this morning when I went above," said Misty aloud. "But, did I have it with me when I went back down? I remember I got distracted just as I was about to fly below... Oh no! I must have left it when I was helping the unicorn!"

She had stopped to help a unicorn who had gotten himself stuck in some wild berry bushes. She felt so sorry for him. The more he moved around trying to get free, the more tangled up he became. Misty calmed him down by singing a song to him. It was the same song her mother used to sing to her when she was upset. Finally, she got his beautiful emerald green mane free and off he flew, spreading his wings and soaring into the sky.

After checking with the unicorn, she knew that he was not able to help her. He had not seen her basket. If he had not seen it, then she had probably left in on the surface. Oh dear, this is what the

Queen had been talking about when she told Misty that all her attention needed to be on her job. An older and wiser Wish Fairy would have calmed the unicorn down and went for help. Now Misty was very worried what the Council was going to say about this.

Back above ground, Hope handed the basket to her mother. "Here it is, Mom. Now you will see how important it is for us to get this back to Misty."

Hope's mom thought for a moment and said, "I agree Hope; I think I know of a way we can do this. You are to ask for a wish. You will say you wish to see the Wish Fairy and tell her that you have found her basket."

"Holy Fairy Dust! What a great idea." Hope said.

"Now, Hope, I do not want you to get too excited, because it may not be as simple as it sounds." Of course, Hope's mom was right.

Misty flew over the beautiful blue pond filled with lily pads, looking for her own mother. She swooped down and sat on one of the beautiful see-through pads. She was looking at her reflection in the water when she started to cry, thinking to herself that maybe she wasn't a good Wish Fairy after all. How could she have let this happen?

Misty looked up to see that her mother had landed on the lily pad next to her. "Misty," her mother said, "The unicorn has told me that you have been looking for me. He said that you have a serious problem that you need to talk to me about."

They talked about her lost basket and then just sat on their lily pads deep in thought. Misty's mother told her that they would figure it out together and not to lose faith.

Hope sat by her window that night looking up at the stars. With all the love in her heart, she whispered into the night air, "Oh, Misty, please grant my wish. It is for you to know that I have found your basket of wishes and want to return it to you."

For a brief moment the stars parted, leaving a clear passage for the moon. She hoped that it was a good sign, but she knew that all she could do now was to wait for some news from Misty. She said her prayers and went to sleep.

The next morning, Misty's mother informed her that there was an important wish that came through the night for her. She was amazed to find out that it was from Hope. Hope had found her wish basket in the wildflower field! Misty's mother told her that the only way she was going to be able to go above and get her basket was to once again appear before the Council.

"I must warn you; this is not going to be easy." The rules were clear. Once a Wish Fairy made a mistake, it had to be cleared by the Council before this fairy was allowed to go above to the surface.

"I know, Mother. I really have to do this if I am ever going to be the Wish Fairy that I want to be." The Council was meeting in the morning, and she wanted more than anything to make things right again. She was nervous all day.

Waking up very early the following morning, Misty knew that soon she would be hearing the trumpet blasts announcing that the Council meeting was about to begin. She wanted to be ready and waiting when the Queen entered the chambers for the meeting.

She arrived just in time to see all the fairies arrive from all over the kingdom. They had heard about Misty's problem, and they all wanted to support her.

The Queen arrived and all was silent. She raised her wand high up into the air and said, "Before we begin our business today, one of our newly appointed Wish Fairies has something she would like to discuss with this Council. Come forward." Misty flew up so that she was standing right in front of the Queen.

Unafraid, she looked right into the Queen's face. "Your Majesty, I have brought a serious problem upon myself. You have given me a position of great importance, and for that I am very grateful. Being a Wish Fairy is the best thing in my life. Perhaps, at first, I did not fully understand what a huge responsibility it is. But I have learned that it takes all of your time, and your mind must be on your job every minute. I have made a terrible mistake. I stopped to help a unicorn on my way down from the surface and lost my basket of wishes."

"Misty, this is quite serious. Do you know where you left it?"

"I do. My friend Hope told me through a wish that she found my basket in the wildflower field right at the point of entry to the kingdom. I must have dropped it when I heard the unicorn call for help."

"Misty, this is not going to be an easy decision for me. We make rules for a reason and we feel that they are fair. You are asking us to let you go above, get your basket and go on with your normal activities. What if your friend Hope had not found your basket? All of those people who asked for a wish to be granted would have thought that you deserted them. None of their wishes would come true. Even worse, what if an evil troll had somehow gotten his hands on it? No, Misty, this is a serious mistake that will not be easily fixed."

"I understand that what I did was very careless, but surely your Highness, is there any Wish Fairy here who has not made one mistake? Will you please let me try to make this right? I want to prove to you and this Council that I will do anything it takes to make you believe in me again."

"You have a pure heart, Misty," said the Queen. "Thank you for speaking so honestly. The Council has much to talk about. You must leave now, but your mother may stay. When the voting begins she will have to leave."

Misty thanked the Council, kissed her mother and flew back to the lily pad where they had talked yesterday. She knew her mother would come and find her there.

Misty's mother was very nervous. She listened as the fairies talked back and forth among themselves. They all remembered the mistakes they made when they were first starting their jobs.

The Council was finished. The time had come for the voting to begin. Unable to vote, Misty's mother flew off to be with her daughter. She knew where Misty would be waiting. Landing on the lily pad and seeing her daughter so upset, she really wanted to comfort her, but secretly she was also very worried about the Council's decision.

Bright and early the next morning, Misty was called to appear at the palace. Many fairies were there to hear the decision. Yesterday, after Misty left, several of the fairies spoke up on her behalf.

One by one they told the Queen about the mistakes they had made. The Council told the Queen that they felt it would be fair to give Misty another chance.

Misty stood in front of the Queen once again and waited for the Queen to speak.

"Misty, this is what we have decided. You must follow our directions very carefully. You must appear to your friend Hope in a dream. Ask her what she thinks is the most important wish in the basket. We know that she is also a true believer at heart, and she would have read the wishes in order to help you. She will awake for a moment and then fall back to sleep. When she dreams, it will be about the wish. Bring this wish back to us, and you will have the rest of your instructions."

When Hope awoke in the middle of that night, she wasn't quite sure what woke her. She fell back to sleep thinking of Francesca and her wish. Misty knew that this was one wish that she would try her hardest to grant, even if it turned out to be her last one.

Misty brought the wish back to the Queen as she was told to do. The Queen felt the wish was very honorable and one that they should grant.

"In order to grant this wish and keep your job as Wish Fairy," said the Queen, "there are certain rules that you must follow.

"Francesca's grandmother's bakery must be rebuilt in time for her to make Virginia's wedding cake. But listen carefully. You must not use magic to rebuild the bakery, and no other Wish Fairy can help you in any way.

"You have all the knowledge you need inside of you to accomplish this. When you have granted this wish, your mother will contact us, and we will have another meeting of the High Council. Do you understand all of this, Misty?"

"I do."

After thanking the Council, the Queen wished her good luck and off she flew back to her palace.

Misty sat for a while, watching the burst of color that the fairies made as they spread their wings and flew into the sky.

Italy was an amazing place with lush green valleys, tall snowcapped mountains and busy cities. Most of all, Misty loved the small village where Francesca and her family lived.

The streets were paved with beautiful, different-colored cobblestones. The small church, with its cool, sweet-smelling lemon trees lining the walk, welcomed people to prayer. Small shops filled the main street, selling many different kinds of goods. The smell of cheese and fish was everywhere, but there was no mistaking the terrible smell that a large fire left. That was where Sophia's bakery burned to the ground.

It was the saddest sight Misty could remember experiencing. She could see several townspeople gathered, all shaking their heads in disbelief.

Misty needed a place to think. She found a beautiful park with a pond. A few small boys were sailing homemade boats across the water, and the sound of their laughter filled the air. She landed on a patch of grass near a shade tree.

The Queen told her that she was able to use any of the suggestions that the Council had offered her. They let her use a dream to find out what Francesca's wish was, so she was also going to use dreams to get the bakery built.

Misty learned that almost everyone in the village had received or bought a cake from Sophia's bakery at least once. In fact, most of the town bought all of their baked goods from her. So she decided to visit several of the villager's dreams to see how they could help.

In her first dream visit, she learned that the mayor of the town had just celebrated his 50th wedding anniversary. Sophia made him and his wife a beautiful cake. It was decorated to look like a pretty winter scene. Sophia placed a park bench on it, just like the one the couple sat on the night that he proposed. The trees on the cake were made of white and dark chocolate, and the icing that she draped over the branches looked like snow with ice crystals on them. Tiny pure white sugar doves surrounded the young happy couple figures that she had placed on the bench. Sophia had given them one of the greatest gifts they had received.

The next dream that Misty visited belonged to the pastor of the village church. He often dreamed about the little orphan boy who came to stay at the parish house one day and never left.

Just before the boy was about to celebrate his eighth birthday, the pastor heard the children talking and discovered the lonely little boy loved the circus so much. The pastor came into the bakery to buy some fresh bread, and he told Sophia about the boy and that the villagers were going to give him a small party in the church hall one week later.

Hearing this, she insisted on making him a very special cake. The next day, Sophia went out to get supplies. She saw the little boy on the street and said, "Good morning, young man. I hear that you are having a birthday soon. I also hear that you like the circus."

"Oh, yes. I sometimes dream at night about all the animals performing and acrobats spinning around on their ropes. I especially like the clowns that make me laugh."

"Well, that is so nice," said Sophia. "I will see you at the party!" He waved, and off down the street he ran. Sophia knew exactly what kind of cake she was going to make.

The morning of the party was bright and clear. Sophia packed up the cake and started her short walk to the church. She loved walking through the church garden to the church hall where the party was to be held. It was a poor church, but you never would have known it. The place was decorated to look just like a circus. She knew that it probably took much of the church's collection money this week to do this. But no one there seemed to mind.

"Where is the birthday boy?" Sophia shouted over the noise of the children playing and running around.

"I'm here," said the cute little boy with the smile that showed that his two front teeth were missing.

"Well, then. This must be for you." Sophia opened the box and a hush fell over the hall. The cake was amazing. It was complete with lions, elephants, clowns and acrobats. Bunches of sugar balloons were on each corner, and in the middle was a moving merry-go-round with horses that twirled round and round. The little boy stood in the middle of the hall with this cake in his hands.

"This is the best birthday I have ever had! Thank you so much! I will never forget you."

As Misty flew around, she could see how the loss of the bakery had made the villagers sad. One of the people who was the most saddened by this was the caretaker who had left the candle burning that night.

He knew that it was his fault that the fire started, and he wished there was some way that he could make it right. Through dream, Misty saw a wonderful memory of the time he first started helping Sophia at the bakery. He found out that his wife was expecting twins. On the day of his children's birth, two identical cakes were delivered to their door, one in pink and one in blue. Beautiful, delicate cakes. He never forgot how happy his wife was. Now to think that he was responsible for losing the bakery was more than he could bear.

The last person that Misty visited in dream was a widow who had the honor of being the mother of the only child in the village to graduate college. The village had a huge graduation celebration, and the whole town had come out to congratulate the young man. Francesca's grandmother made the biggest cake she had ever made. It was fit for a king.

Of course Sophia would take no money, because she felt it was an honor to bake it. She was so proud of him, and this was her way of showing him how proud she was.

After Misty's visits, everyone went to sleep with the same thought. The little Wish Fairy had given the town the push they needed.

They all needed to remember how important Sophia and her bakery were to this town.

The next day, the whole village was in an uproar. The mayor called a town meeting and asked everyone to attend. The villagers knew why they were there. The mayor needed their help. They were going to have to stick together and come up with a way to rebuild the bakery. The villagers wanted to do it for Sophia, to pay her back for all the kindness that she had shown them through the years.

The mayor stood up and said, "My dear townspeople, we are all in agreement about what needs to be done. I know, of course, that we are a poor village with no spare money. It is up to us to figure out what we can do to help." One by one the people took turns telling the mayor their ideas. No time could be wasted if the bakery was going to be rebuilt in time for Sophia's granddaughter's wedding.

The villagers did not have much, but whatever extra they could spare they gave to the bakery fund. Word about what the town was doing and why spread out to other villages. Money and donations started coming in from all over. But even when they counted all the money that everyone had generously given, they knew that it would not be nearly enough to rebuild the bakery. Everyone went home that night with a sad heart and an extra prayer on their lips.

Misty had been keeping a watchful eye on what was going on in the village. She had been so happy when all the donations started coming in, but now she was worried. These poor people, she thought; they have fought so hard for Francesca and her grandmother. Never once did she hear them complain about not having enough money for themselves. She had to think of something else to help these villagers raise money.

Misty remembered something that she had seen in one of the dreams. The widow had been dreaming about her son, Franco, who graduated from college. Franco loved to build things. As a child his favorite toy was the hammer his father had given him. They were very poor and didn't have a lot of money for toys, but Franco didn't mind. He loved to build birdhouses and little toy boats out of the scraps of wood he would find.

As he grew, he would walk around the village, fixing things that the villagers didn't have the money to pay a carpenter for. Someone would always have a creaky stair or a broken window.

He made himself a promise that he would work hard and go to school. He would have a fancy toolbox with everything he would need in it. Franco would build beautiful houses for people to live in and big buildings for them to work in. He wanted to be successful and make his village proud.

When he went off to school, the people all chipped in some money and bought him a small toolbox. He still uses those tools as a reminder of what those people sacrificed for him. So many of Franco's dreams had come true. He went to bed almost every night thinking of ways to repay them for their kindness to him.

This was the perfect chance for Misty to send her message to Franco in his dreams. She told him of the problem in the village.

The young man was deeply troubled when he awoke the next morning after this terrible nightmare. He saw the bakery going up in flames and Francesca and her grandmother crying. He had tossed and turned all night. He decided to take a ride to his mother's village and see for himself what was going on there.

He got into his truck and carefully placed the toolbox that the villagers had given him inside. Off he went. Franco drove all through the night and the next day, just stopping long enough to eat.

When he arrived in the village, it was just getting dark. Everyone rushed out to greet him. His mother hugged him tight and said, "Oh, Franco, I cannot believe my eyes. Is it really you?"

"Yes, mother, I had a terrible dream. There was a lot of sadness here. I have come to make sure that everything is alright."

They invited Franco into the town hall where they talked long into the night. The mayor told him of the problem and how they did the best they could but did not raise the money to rebuild Sophia's bakery.

"My dear friends, all of you helped me become what I am today. If it were not for you, I could not have finished school. You taught me something I could never have learned in any school. These things are honesty, loyalty, faithfulness, generosity and, most of all, love. I will rebuild the bakery for Sophia, and I will do it in time for the wedding." The people of the village rejoiced.

Franco had much to do. He needed to make many phone calls. He needed many materials to be delivered to the village and asked many men to help with the building. Secretly, he hoped that he had not made a promise that he was not going to be able to keep.

What Franco did not know was that he had a hidden good luck charm. He had the Wish Fairy herself watching over him! She couldn't use her magic, but sometimes just a little bit of fairy dust helped keep things moving along.

Meanwhile, Hope was beginning to wonder if she was ever going to hear any news from Misty. Hope knew that she would just have to keep wishing and hoping that soon she would have the answers she wanted.

As soon as the sun was up the next morning, the village was alive with the sounds of large trucks and men talking and shouting orders. The old bakery was too far gone, and a bulldozer had to knock it down.

As days passed, the villagers watched in amazement as the bakery began to take shape. It was going to be beautiful. Franco would make sure that it looked as much like the old bakery as possible, even though the inside of the bakery would have all of the modern conveniences. Shiny new ovens would replace the old rusty ones, and everything Sophia could want and need for baking would be there. It would be magnificent.

Sophia refused to watch the new bakery being built. She wanted to wait until it was finished, as she could not believe that Franco was doing this for her. Soon she would be baking again! She felt in her heart that it was her granddaughter Francesca's wish that had made this possible.

One night, after the bakery had burned down, she went to check on Francesca before bed and heard her making the wish. She was so overwhelmed. She quietly slipped into her own room, her heart filled with love.

And then, the big day finally arrived. The bakery was finished! Franco wanted to be the one to show Sophia her new bakery, so he went to her home to pick her up. The workmen had tied a huge red bow and attached it to the front door. Everyone waited with much excitement for Sophia to arrive.

When Sophia, Francesca, her mother, father and the twins arrived, everyone in the village was there. Tears poured down Sophia's face. When she could finally talk, she said "Franco, my dear family and friends, how can I ever thank you for what you have given me today?"

Franco replied, "Sophia, there is no need to thank me. What you have given all of us should take a lifetime to repay. Just be happy and bake your granddaughter's wedding cake. I hope that you will bake cakes for us for many years to come."

Sophia settled into her new bakery with not much time to spare. She set right to work on the wedding cake that she had been dreaming about.

Francesca was right there with her every step of the way. After all, Sophia wanted to teach Francesca to be the best baker in the village, and Francesca wanted to learn all her grandmother's baking secrets. She wanted to learn all she could so she could take over for her grandmother when it became too hard for her.

Misty didn't realize that she had granted two wishes that day— Francesca's and Sophia's. Sophia had been wishing that her granddaughter would follow in her footsteps.

The wedding day was finally here. The bride was beautiful, the groom was handsome and the cake was fabulous. Sophia insisted that something magical had guided her hands that day. The frosting flowers looked like they had just been picked from the finest garden. The white sugar doves looked so real that you could imagine them flying off the cake and into the sky.

The celebration went on and on. As the happy couple was leaving for their honeymoon, the air was filled with a soft swishing sound. "What is that noise?" everyone asked.

"Oh, it's probably just the wind," said Sophia. Francesca smiled and looked up to heaven. She knew that the sound was magical. Her wish had been granted, and her Wish Fairy was returning to her home.

Francesca was right. Misty had completed her mission, and she now had to return to the palace to talk to the Queen.

She flew home very happy. Her happiness did not come from the thought of her being able to keep her job, but from the thought of that little girl getting her wish.

She flew directly to the palace. "I must speak to her Royal Highness at once please," she told the gatekeeper. The Queen had actually already been informed by Misty's mother that the wish had been granted and that the little fairy was on her way to see her.

The Queen flew into the throne room. "I am glad that you have returned to us safe and sound. Tell me about your trip and everything that has happened since we last talked."

After Misty finished the story, the Queen told her to go out to the meadow where she was sure everyone had now gathered and to wait. Her mother was the first to reach her. She kissed Misty and welcomed her home.

The Queen appeared shortly and said, "Misty, the Council and I have decided that you have shown what a good Wish Fairy you are. You did a wonderful job in granting that little girl's wish. Therefore, I give you permission to go to the surface and get your basket of wishes. But do not appear to Hope again until she asks you to grant a wish." This was okay, because Misty knew how she would thank Hope.

The next morning Hope woke up with a feeling that something good was going to happen. She sat up in bed and rubbed her eyes. Holy Fairy Dust! Written on her mirror in silver glitter were the simple words:

Thank You Hope—until we meet again—
Love, Misty.

Hope looked over to where she had kept Misty's basket every minute since she found it. Sure enough, it was gone. She was so happy. Misty had her basket back, and her fairy friend was safe and sound!

Hope thought to herself that life was good, and it didn't hurt that she had a Wish Fairy as a best friend either!

Holy Fairy Dust !

Turn the page for a peek
at another exciting
adventure of

Misty the Wish Fairy

and her friend Hope

The Wish Fairy

The Cottage Down the Lane
with the Dragon Out Back

Hope was a dreamer. She looked at things differently. For one thing she had a best friend in Misty, who was not only a fairy, but a Wish Fairy. Hope and Misty had many wonderful adventures together.

Lately Hope had really been worried about her friend Misty. She went to see her mom who was making Hope's favorite snack—double chocolate chip brownies. "Mom," said Hope, "I am pretty worried about Misty. She has not been around for a while, and I really miss her flying around my pillow early in the morning."

"Well, Hope, when was the last time you sensed she was around?" Mom asked.

"Last week. She left a message and said she couldn't wait to visit the new kid that lived in the cottage down the lane."

"Alright, Hope, try not to worry too much. Have some brownies. Maybe you could go visit and see if there is any sign of Misty. I haven't met the child yet, but at the grocery store the other day I met his mother. We talked for a while and I invited them over for a visit. She said that would be nice and she would be in touch. And you would be able to tell if Misty had been there by the way the grass was bent or by the fairy dust she leaves on the flowers."

After thinking for a while about what her mom said, Hope decided that she was right. She would go visit the new kid and find out all she could about her Wish Fairy friend Misty.

It was a beautiful day for a walk. She knew the fairies had been very busy this morning because the flowers were especially colorful and three butterflies flew by her with newly painted wings. The leaves of the trees had a beautiful golden glow, which meant the leaf fairies had not yet collected the gold dust that the stars had left from the night before. She knew all this because she had seen what the fairies do when she attended the meeting with the Council of Fairies. It had taken place in a beautiful wildflower field with thousands of fairies. Hope had been allowed to attend because she needed to save her friend and prove to the Council that Misty would be a good Wish Fairy. This brought back a lot of memories for Hope, and it made her want to find out what happened to her friend, and fast.

As she got closer to the cottage, Hope wrinkled her nose at the strange, sweet smell coming from the cottage chimney. It was not unpleasant, just strange. It was like nothing she had ever smelled before. She noticed a pink glow surrounding the place and birds of every shape, size and color just gliding through the air. It was positively magical.

She knew in her heart that Misty had something to do with this cottage, and Hope just needed to find out what it was.

For more information about

Misty the Wish Fairy

and her friend Hope

visit

www.sandrareilly.com

and remember to always

BELIEVE !

About the Author

Sandra has been creating and telling stories to her children and grandchildren for many years. From scary stories around a campfire to heart-warming bedtime stories, she has instilled the belief in magic to many young minds.

Her goal is to not only get children to read, but more importantly to see and feel the magic found within the pages.

Sandra was born and raised in Utica, New York, and currently lives there with her husband Jeff. Her life, centered around family and friends, is full of magical times and magical food!

About the Illustrator

Dominique has her Masters of Science by Research degree from the University of New South Wales, Australia and is currently pursuing her doctorate in Chemistry.

She lives in upstate New York.